SECRETS OF A FORTNITE FAN

LAST SQUAD STANDING

Published in 2021 by Mortimer Children's Books Limited
An imprint of the Welbeck Publishing Group
20 Mortimer Street, London W1T 3JW
Text and illustration © Welbeck Publishing Limited,
part of Welbeck Publishing Group
ISBN: 978 1 83935 053 5

This book is not endorsed by Epic Games, Inc. All images of Fortnite
characters/gameplay © Epic Games, Inc.

Writer: Eddie Robson
Illustrator: Oscar Herrero
Designer: Melinda Penn
Design Manager: Matt Drew
Editorial Manager: Joff Brown
Production: Rachel Burgess

A catalogue record for this book is available from the British Library.

Printed in the UK
10 9 8 7 6 5 4 3 2 1

All game information correct as of April 2021

Disclaimer: This book is a guide book for general informational
purposes only and should not be relied upon revealing or
recommending any specific direct secrets and methods of the game.
The publisher and the author are not associated with any names,
characters, trademarks, service marks and trade names referred to
herein, which are the property of their respective owners and are used
solely for identification purposes. This book is a publication of Welbeck
Children's Limited and has not been licensed, approved, sponsored, or
endorsed by any person or entity.

SECRETS OF A FORTNITE FAN

LAST SQUAD STANDING

EDDIE ROBSON

CHAPTER 1

I'm running through the woods, which is giving me some cover but not enough. I need to make a choice and I need to make it quickly: do I hide out here, or keep going and hope I can stay ahead of the danger?

I can hear footsteps echoing off the trees. Who am I kidding - they're catching up with me.

If I don't do something soon it'll be too late. I dive into a nearby bush...

But there's someone already hiding there!

"Tyler! What are you doing?" says the person in the bush. It's Leon.

"Move over," I say, ducking down and tucking my legs under myself so my shoes can't be seen sticking out.

"This is my hiding place."

"There's enough room for both of us."

"They'll see us both."

"They'll hear us both if you don't shut up - they're coming!"

Leon listens, and he realises I'm right - you can hear their feet pounding through the forest, coming our way.

"This is like something from Fortnite," whispers Leon, grinning.

"Shut up," I reply, peeking through the branches...

Here they come. The school track team.

They always do this when we have a cross-country run. They hang back for the first ten minutes, jogging slowly, to let everyone else get ahead.

Then, bam, they start running - and it's like they have a competition going to see how many of the other kids they can trip or knock over.

In fact I think they literally *do* have a competition going, so the best strategy is to hide before they reach you.

Of course the worst thing is if they find you hiding - then they'll make fun of you for hiding until you start running again, and then they trip you up.

**Leon and I both hold our breath...
...and they run straight past. Less than a metre from us.**

"Close call," murmurs Leon as they thunder away into the woods.

We stand up, get back on the path and start running.

"Imagine if this was Fortnite," Leon says. "We could lay a fire trap for them. Imagine that. Or make a sniper nest over there and –"

"Leon," I say, "instead of talking about Fortnite, can we just hurry up so I can get home and play Fortnite?"

OK, let me catch you up a bit. Leon's my mate, but he's also kind of my arch-nemesis in Fortnite. And outside Fortnite.

Leon and I had this big rivalry thing going when I was still a noob, but I teamed up with a couple of our

TYLER

SANA

ELLIE

ALFIE

other friends, Sana and Ellie, and Alfie (my slightly weird mate who goes to a different school) and we Victory Royale'd him.

Anyway, since then he's kind of respected me, a bit, maybe? But I know he also wants to get his revenge on me, so he's been frustrated that I haven't been playing Fortnite lately.

So he looks quite excited when I mention I'm going to play when I get home.

"Oh," he says, "have your mum and dad lifted the ban?"

"I wasn't banned from playing Fortnite."

"They said you couldn't play any more. Sounds like you were banned to me."

"No, I *agreed* –"

I don't get to finish this sentence because something's just hit me from behind, and I'm too busy falling face first in the mud.

"What hit me?" I say as Leon helps me up.

"Amy," says Leon – and as I look up, there's Amy,

vanishing into the distance, her feet pounding the
ground.

"She could have at least said sorry."

But that's Amy. She never apologises for anything.
Or says anything at all, really. Most of us are too
scared to talk to her.

"Anyway," I say as we start running again, "I wasn't banned from playing Fortnite. What happened, was I agreed to take a one-month break."

"Yeah right, it was all your idea."

"It was! Sort of."

What happened was that I got a little bit behind on school stuff, and Mum and Dad thought Fortnite was distracting me.

I told them I could prove it wasn't anything to do with Fortnite by catching up while playing exactly the same amount.

It would be like a scientific experiment!

Mum and Dad suggested a slightly different plan where I stopped playing Fortnite for a month, and if my grades improved I could start again.

So you see, it was my own idea. Partly.

Anyway, my grades are up, and if they stay that way I can keep playing.

I already checked for updates yesterday, and I even

downloaded and installed them so I don't have to wait around for them before I start playing.

I'm feeling pretty pleased about how smart that was - I can't wait to get back in the game.

Alfie knows I've been waiting for this and I know he'll be waiting for me in the lobby.

(Alfie got into Fortnite about the same time as me, but he's got a pretty unusual way of playing. He doesn't like violence and his parents don't approve of games where you go around shooting people - so Alfie has NEVER actually fired a weapon in the game!)

Finally I get home and turn the console on.

Oh yes! I am BACK, baby!

I was right. Alifie is waiting for me and ready to go.

But hang on a minute...

Alfie's obviously been playing a lot while I've been away - his XP level is 43!

There's no way this can be right... Somehow my XP is...

CHAPTER 2
SEASON 6
LEVEL 1

MeekerSeeker88

1?!?

NO WAY! I was on about 68 last time I played.

"Where'd all my XP go?" I say into the microphone.

"Yeah... They reset all the XP scores at the start of each season," Alfie tells me.

Oh man. I'M A NOOB AGAIN.

But I remind myself, - I'm not really a noob, I've got skills. In fact, maybe this is good - other people will underestimate me if they think I'm a noob.

And I'll get that level up in no time.

Alfie and I launch into a Duos match, I bring up the map... but, hang on, this is all wrong.

"Er, Alfie?"

"Yeah?" he replies.

"What happened to the map?"

It's the same map, but there's loads of dark areas with question marks on them - places I know I've been to.

"New season," says Alfie.

"Can we go somewhere I know? Just while I find my way around?"

"Sure."

I head for a spot that's always quiet and filled with loot. The place where I've landed looks the same as ever, but there's usually a chest there, and there's nothing. I check the next room... and there's nothing there either!

Immediately everything goes wrong!

"I can't find any weapons! Help!" I shout to Alfie.

"Oh yeah, there's not as much loot around since the update."

"Why didn't you tell me that?"

"What would you have done if I had?"

This is exactly the kind of annoying thing Alfie says, and it's particularly annoying because I never know how to reply.

And I'm getting a little frustrated about how much Alfie seems to know. I mean, if it wasn't for me, he'd never even have started playing Fortnite!

I'm the one who convinced him he could play without shooting and now... weirdly... it really seems to be working for him.

Alfie got a Victory Royale in his first ever match, and he really played his part when we beat Leon, so I'm not really complaining.

It's good to have a friend who it as into Fortnite as you are - but if I'm honest, I am a bit annoyed that Alfie is the expert, not me!

I'm still trying to think of what on earth to do next when a volley of gunfire comes from the screen and my avatar's knocked down.

What... There's someone else here?!

I wasn't expecting that!

There's never anyone else here...

I get that Fortnite updates are important to help keep the game fresh, but at this moment I'm not too happy at how much a new season can throw you off.

Strategies that used to work suddenly don't any more, weapons you'd mastered aren't in the game - and everyone else is playing differently too, so you have to get used to that.

If - like me - you're new to an update and you want to explore changes to the map, or try out a new weapon, a Battle Labs session lets you take the time to do it.

I need Battle Labs RIGHT NOW!

If you are going into Battle Labs, why not invite some friends - it's always more fun with friends, plus that way you've got people to shoot.

When I was first getting into Fortnite, Alfie was my guinea pig in Battle Labs - I shot him hundreds of times just to get the hang of things and he didn't mind at all!

But when you get into a real match, it's good to play cautiously at first - watch what other players do and where they land.

You've probably noticed that the Fortnite map includes one or more loot strongholds, which include Mythical weapons that you can't get anywhere else.

These are guarded by NPCs (non-playable characters) and you have to take them down if you want to get at the weapons.

There's usually a boss guarding the loot (a boss is an NPC who will fight you!)

A lot of players jump off the bus and head straight for these loot strongholds, desperate to be the first to grab the Mythical weapons.

After an update there'll be new loot strongholds and new bosses, so watch out for changes in how and where people land.

Your approach to loot strongholds and your landing tactics will depend a lot on how you like to play the game.

Which is more important to you: having fun, or WINNING?

A lot of the early eliminations in a match happen around these popular strongholds, because you've got lots of players and NPCs scrapping it out.

So there's a high chance that stuff will go badly wrong.

For example, you might be lucky enough to battle your way to the prized loot, but take so much damage on the way, that someone else can just walk up behind you, kill you and take it from you.

So is it worth it?

Well, it is pretty exciting if you get that top loot and eliminating someone with a Mythical weapon lets them know you're someone to be reckoned with.

But how much difference does it make to your chances of winning?

Honestly, not that much.

Most of my Victory Royales happened because I hit on a good strategy, or because I used the weapons I had well, not because I had awesome weapons.

(Having said that, one time I did win by taking out someone's fort with a grenade launcher. That was COOL.)

If you do pick up something special from one of these strongholds, remember you don't have to use it.

It might not be the best weapon for the job.

Don't use a legendary sniper rifle if a basic grenade will be more effective!

I'm not obsessed with getting the best loot and I'd really prefer to avoid the carnage early on, so I've found it's not a bad idea to land around the edges of the map where there are usually fewer strongholds.

And if you used to have a favourite spot that always had lots of chests, there's a good chance it's been targeted in an update to weaken it!

It sucks, but you'll have to find somewhere new.

The main thing I realised is, don't let all the updates

throw you off too much. Players get excited by anything new in the game and want to try it out - but underneath it all, the game is the same. Once you've adapted to the new stuff, most of your old strategies will still work and if some new element doesn't fit the way you play, you don't have to use it!

CHAPTER 2

"You want to play a match tonight?" asks Leon, leaning on my desk at school.

I'm wishing I hadn't mentioned I was getting back into playing Fortnite when I spoke to him the other day.

After an epic Battle Labs session the other night with Alfie, I've been playing every spare chance I get between homework and chores.

I've managed to build up my XP level a bit, but it's still in single figures, and I want to get it up a bit higher before I play a match with Leon.

Even if we're playing on the same squad, he'll want to prove he's a better player than me, and there's no way I can let him get away with THAT.

I just need a bit more time to get the hang of the game again, tweak my strategy and stuff.

"Think I'm too busy," I say.

"What are you busy with?" Leon says, grinning. "Don't tell me you've got a secret girlfriend?"

Luckily I don't have to answer this because our new teacher, Ms Grimes, walks in.

"Leon, stop leaning on Tyler's desk please," she says.

"Whose desk would you like me to lean on, Ms Grimes?" says Leon innocently.

Ms Grimes' eyes narrow. "Sit down, Leon. In your chair, before you treat us to some other hilarity."

She explains that today we're starting a new Design and Technology project, and we all have to make an object with some kind of mechanical element.

"It could be a tower with an elevator, or a bridge that opens to let boats through..." she says.

"Or a school with a trapdoor that leads to a dungeon for kids who won't behave!" Ellie interrupts.

This is the way Ellie's mind usually works - she's the most aggressive Fortnite player I know, and she really enjoys laying a good trap.

Ms Grimes nods. She seems to quite like this idea too.

In fact, she is smiling with a sort of faraway look in her eyes for a few moments, before she snaps back at us.

"Now," Ms Grimes continues, "you're going to do this in groups of four..."

Immediately there's an outburst of chatter as everyone agrees who they're going to be in a group with.

I glance over at Sana, and she nods.

Sana's good with mechanical stuff, she fixed my scooter once - and also she's cool, and taught me pretty much everything I know about Fortnite, so of course I want to be in her group.

Ms Grimes tells us to be quiet.

"I will choose the groups. I've made sure there's a mix of skills in each team. There will be no swapping between the groups."

So Sana gets put in a group with Leon - typical.

"And Tyler," Ms Grimes says, pointing at me, "you're with Maisie, Samson and Amy."

What?!!

I don't think it's possible to be put in a worse group than this one.

Leon looks over at me and winks.

By the end of the first session, we're meant to have some ideas about what we're going to build.

But instead of working on a proper idea, Maisie spends the whole time testing out different team names and designing logos, while Samson tells her it doesn't matter.

Amy becomes obsessed with trying to catch a spider.

It's clear this is not going to work out well.

We're supposed to brainstorm ideas when we get home - but after the day I've had, I feel like I just need to unwind with some Fortnite first.

And Ellie's suggestion has reminded me, I really need to get better at traps...

Traps can be very satisfying it they are used well, and I would like nothing better than to see Leon's face when he walks straight into one of mine.

Traps are more common in the old Save The World version of Fortnite - they're an important part of defending your fort from zombies.

In Save the World you can plant traps around the base of your fort and catch zombies before they can reach the walls, and you can also plant them inside, to attack them if they get in.

Traps don't get used as much in Battle Royale - in fact, while there are loads of different traps in Save The World, they keep getting put in the vault in Battle Royale, so you have far less choice.

But because traps don't get used as much, your opponents are less likely to be looking out for them - and you can use that to your advantage.

There are lots of different ways you can use traps, but remember that they need to be planted on particular surfaces - you always need a flat built surface - it can't just be any piece of ground.

Also, when placing your trap make sure you know what the range is.

Your opponent won't always need to stand directly on a trap to activate it - sometimes a trap will be activated when someone just gets close to it.

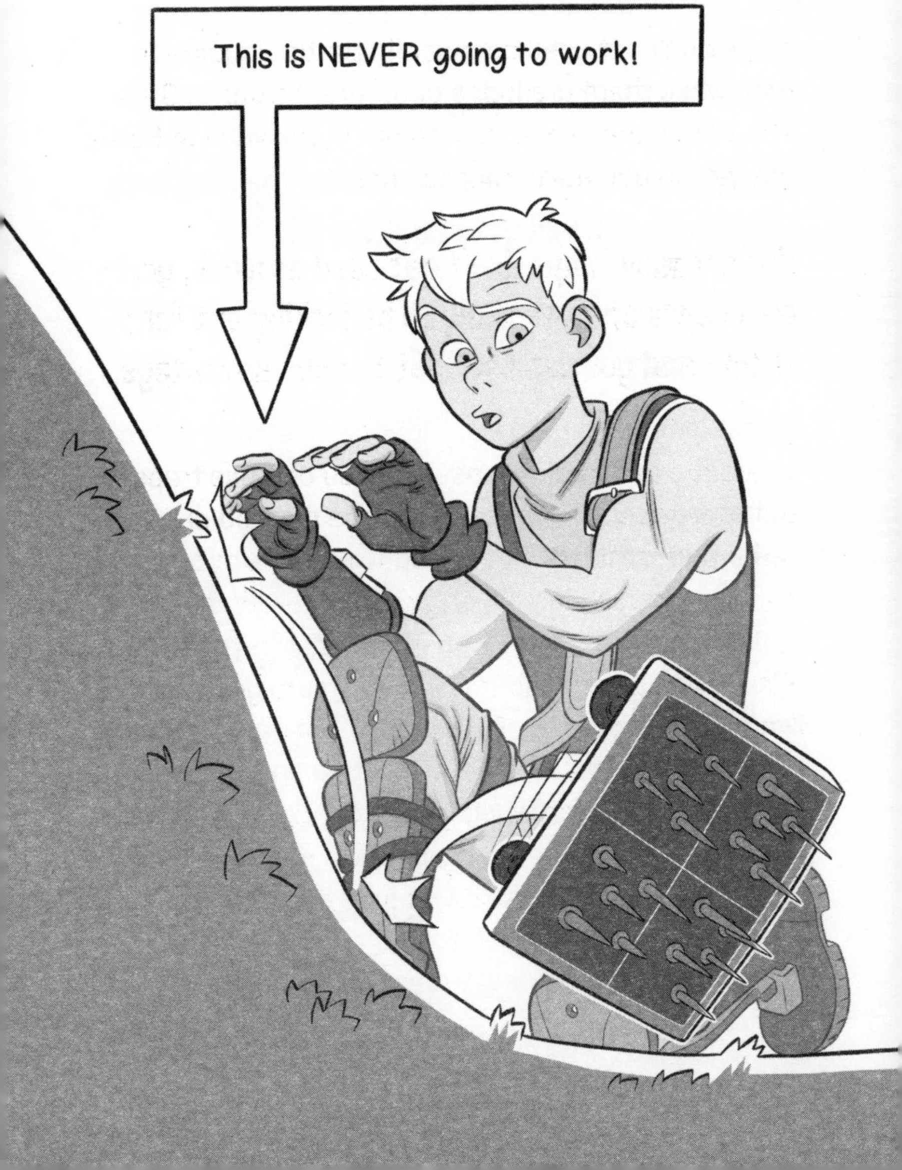
This is NEVER going to work!

The most obvious thing to do is plant a trap as part of your fort - just outside the entrance can work, or even just inside the entrance.

Or if you want to be more tricky you could build a stairway around the outside of your fort and then place the trap at the bottom...

Any opponent who tries to rush up the stairway and attack you will get caught in it!

You can even use traps when building a stand-alone ramp to give yourself a combat advantage.

Sometimes while you're on your ramp shooting at one opponent, another member of their squad will sneak up behind you. If you've placed a trap at the bottom of the ramp, this will put a stop to those tactics!

You can even place a trap on an empty fort.

During the endgame players will often come across a fort which is inside the storm circle and seems to be abandoned – and they'll want to take this fort for themselves.

If you find one of these it can be a perfect trap location - simply place a trap and then hide somewhere nearby.

If you want to be really sneaky, just put up a few walls yourself, so that it looks like someone was building a fort when attacked - that might be enough to lure someone in to using it as a foundation for their own fort.

And BANG they will have walked straight into your cleverly placed trap!

Or if you don't have time to build your own fort, how about putting a trap in your opponent's fort?

If you manage to sneak up to your opponent's fort while they're at the top, you can place a trap outside their door or on their ground floor - then try to tempt them down.

A lot of players will come down if they hear someone clattering around inside their fort - if you need to attract their attention, just start bashing down their walls.

If you know other players will go to a particular spot - like a loot stronghold for example - you can set a trap for them.

If you're the first one to get there, or if the stronghold looks like it'll stay inside the storm circle for a while, then why not lay a trap for any future opponents?

After all, there's often more loot in some of these places than you can possibly carry, and a well-placed trap at the door will:

- **do damage to any other player who comes near**
- **protect you from attack while you're tooling up**
- **stop them picking up the loot you've left behind**

Some players combine the trap with the harpoon gun for a spectacular approach.

If you're in an open space where a combat situation is about to occur, plant a trap on the ground in front of you, then be ready with the harpoon gun.

When your opponent appears, aim for their chest (hitting someone from range with a harpoon is tricky so go for the bigger target).

Reel them in and you'll drag them right over the trap!

But as someone who likes to camp out in buildings, my favourite way to use traps is to plant one just inside the door of where I'm hiding.

Obviously this doesn't mean you're completely safe, as someone might smash through the wall.

But most players will just use the door - especially if you 'stupidly' leave it open so they can see you in there.

You can even try tempting them in by making noises - try swapping and reloading your weapons until someone notices and comes after you.

CHAPTER 3

Next day our group gets together to decide what we're going to build. We all agreed to come up with ideas overnight and bring them in today.

I sort of forgot because I was (ahem) busy last night, but I came up with this over breakfast: a ski lodge on a mountain, and a chair lift that takes you back up to the lodge after you ski down.

(Yeah I got the idea from the ziplines in Fortnite, so what?)

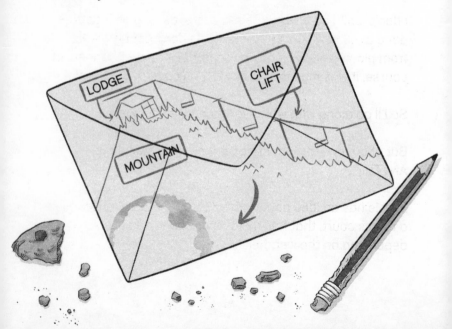

I sit down on a table opposite Amy.

"Morning," I say.

Amy gives me a weird look. "Are you talking to me?"

"Er... yeah."

She laughs like this is the dumbest thing she's ever heard, then goes back to doing what she was doing, which is pushing the point of a compass through the eyes of the people on the cover of her French textbook over and over again.

"So," I say, "what's your idea for the building project?"

Amy shrugs without looking up. She doesn't look up when Maisie and Samson arrive and sit down either.

I don't really care what the project is, as long as it gets done and I get a decent grade and I don't get banned from playing Fortnite again (not that I was ever banned, of course, it was my idea to take a break as I said before).

So I'll go along with whatever the others decide.

But of course, this depends on the others deciding ANYTHING!

Maisie has an idea about making a sports arena, like a tennis court, that has a roof that opens and closes depending on the weather.

Samson hates all sport and refuses to go along with this idea. He wants to make a factory with a conveyor belt.

Like in a Roblox tycoon game?" I say.

"I don't want to do something based on a computer game," says Maisie.

"It's not based on a computer game," says Samson.

"It sounds boring anyway. Factories are boring."

"Everything you use is made in factories! Sport's much more boring!"

I try to show them my ski lodge idea, thinking it might combine the two - it's got sport and the chair lift is like a conveyor belt.

But they both say it's a stupid idea and they don't want to build a mountain and then go back to arguing.

I turn and ask Amy, "What was your idea?"

The other two don't hear me, they're too busy arguing.

Amy opens her exercise book and I peer over at it to see what she's got, hoping it might be some idea that everyone can agree on.

The page is blank.

Amy tears out the page and stuffs it in her mouth.

She chews it a bit.

Then she spits it out so it lands SPLAT on Samson's face.

"What did you do that for?" wails Samson.

Maisie's laughing - but Amy's already torn out another page and is chewing that, and she spits that one at Maisie.

Samson and Maisie fight back, throwing pencils, books, calculators - anything that comes to hand.

If there's one thing Fortnite has taught me it's that hiding out and steering clear of the battle is sometimes the best way to stay in the game!

And in Fortnite, you're at your most vulnerable when your weapon runs out of ammo.

Quick! Reload! Reload! Arrghh!

If this happens, you can grab some cover or keep on the move while you reload - or you can switch to another weapon that's already loaded.

Switching weapons is a standard technique that top players use a lot - while you hesitate, they go on shooting. It will be a lot easier to switch between weapons if you keep similar types next to each other in your inventory.

Make sure they're weapons that work well together – you don't want to switch from a pistol to a sniper rifle when the enemy's just a few metres away.

(The assault rifle is a good weapon to have – it works well at several ranges, so you can use it alongside a weapon like the machine gun or shotgun.)

Practise switching weapons quickly the moment you run out of ammo.

Even better, get to know how much ammo your favourite weapons hold, so you know when they're going to run out.

Some players even master the double-weapon technique, where you carry two of the same weapon so you can switch between them smoothly – you don't even have to adjust to a different type of gun.

The double shotgun is a popular choice with players who do this. The shotgun's a powerful weapon but needs regular reloading, so packing two means you can deal a lot of damage quickly.

This does mean giving over two of your inventory slots to the same weapon, but if shooting is really your thing - like Ellie - then why not find the weapon that works best for it and carry two of those!

Remember to use the weapons that work best for you, rather than the best weapons you find. It's always exciting to find a Legendary weapon, but you don't have to carry it if it's one you don't really like using.

If your typical tactics suit the machine gun best, carrying an Uncommon machine gun might be better than adapting your style of play just so you can use the Epic assault rifle you've found.

But bear in mind that whatever weapons you don't carry, you'll have to leave lying around for others to pick up...

One of the other things I have found out about is crosshair bloom - have you heard of that?

It's an important part of Fortnite combat.

When you're shooting, the bullets that you fire can end up anywhere inside the circle at the centre of your crosshairs.

Looking at this tells you how accurate the weapon you're using is.

The smaller the circle, the more likely it is that bullets will hit the target.

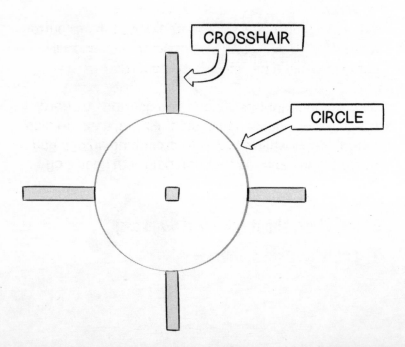

But the circle also changes depending on what you're doing.

Jumping and running around makes the circle get bigger, so your bullets will hit over a wider area.

Of course, moving around can be a really important tactic during battles - standing still makes you an easy target - so I'm not saying you shouldn't move.

But it's good to know what the downside is.

The size of the target circle shrinks if you stand still and aim in.

(So in case you've ever wondered what the point of aiming in is - it increases accuracy!)

It's also a smart idea to repeatedly tap the fire button instead of holding it down - for some reason, this seems to help a bit with overall accuracy.

If your opponent hasn't seen you yet and you don't need to move quickly to avoid their fire, you can also crouch down while shooting - crouching means you move around less, so that can help with accuracy too.

Shoot first, shoot once, I always say!

CHAPTER 4

The rest of my group are in detention for fighting. But I'm not.

Samson and Maisie are furious - they've never had detentions before. And somehow they're all annoyed with me, as if I got out of it in some sneaky way. But all I did was hide under the table and think about Fornite!

You can't put someone in detention for hiding under a table!

So after school, I dump my bag at home and go over to see Alfie - he's my go-to when I need to blow off steam about whatever dumb stuff is going on at school.

Alfie doesn't really know any of my school friends - they've played Fortnite together a few times, but that's it. They probably don't even know what he looks like in real life.

I knock on Alfie's door. His dad answers and tells me Alfie's already got a friend round, but I can go on up. Huh? I didn't know Alfie had other friends?

Alfie's door is open and he's sitting at his desk so I walk straight in, cheerfully saying "Stop what you're doing and listen to what the idiots at my school did today."

"I hope you're not talking about me," comes a voice from the other side of the room.

Sitting on Alfie's bed, eating a plate of toast, is Ellie.

I feel like I've walked into an ambush.

(There's a Fortnite lesson: no matter how familiar a room is, never assume you know what's inside.)

"Oh," I say, "no, not you Ellie – I meant my group for this stupid construction project."

"Oh yeah, that was hilarious," says Ellie. "I already told Alfie about that."

Alfie agrees it's hilarious. But now I don't know what to say.

There's nowhere to sit and Alfie's being quieter than usual, and I keep thinking - why's Ellie got toast? No-one ever offers me toast when *I'm* round.

"So what're you doing here, Ellie?" I ask.

"Didn't you tell him?" Ellie asks Alfie.

"I thought you would," Alfie replies.

"Tell me what?"

"We're entering a tournament," says Ellie.

"What - a Fortnite tournament?"

"It's not likely to be a golf tournament, is it?" laughs Ellie, and Alfie laughs with her.

At me.

"It's not a big tournament," Alfie adds. "But there is a cash prize for the winner."

"So we're talking strategy," Ellie says.

"But... why you two?" I ask.

Ellie shrugs. "While you weren't playing, we got a partnership going. It works. You know I could never be bothered with building."

I turn to Alfie. "So you're still sticking to this no-killing thing?"

"Yeah," says Alfie. "Anyway Ellie's such a good shot, so she concentrates on that -"

"And he looks out for enemies, and I cover him while he's getting supplies, and he works out where we should go," finishes Ellie.

"Weird," I say.

But actually it does sound like a good system, and I'm jealous I don't fit into it.

I'm not as good at shooting as Ellie and I'm not as good at building as Alfie.

"Well, suppose I'd better let you get on with it then."

I say this hoping one of them will say it's fine, I can hang out here. But they don't, so I decide I'd better go. I really didn't expect to find her there, which gets me thinking about ambushes.

Remember, an ambush can happen anywhere.

Avoiding the ambush is an important skill in Fortnite, especially if you're playing against really good, patient players who don't rush into combat.

It's much easier for opponents to pull off an ambush

if you're playing the game in a very predictable way. They can literally see you coming...

And yeah, sometimes it's hard not to play in a predictable way - if you explore a building you naturally want to look in all the rooms, and if you eliminate an opponent you want to pick up their loot.

Aahhh!! Look at this lovely loot!

But remember that when you do the obvious thing, you're more vulnerable to an ambush. Either avoid the obvious, or be extra careful when you're doing it.

Throw up walls and watch out for gunfire!

If you need to explore a building, but want to avoid getting ambushed, try exploring from the top down.

Just build stairs to the roof - or use some kind of launcher, if you've got one - and explore downwards, as if you've just landed.

This can be a good way to take out players who are camping out. Watch out though - once you've built the stairs, anyone else can use them and play your own trick on you!

This tip may come in especially useful if the endgame takes place around buildings.

Sometimes you arrive and you know there are only a few players left, but you can't see anyone. Either they haven't got there yet - or they're already there, but they're hiding.

Don't risk going in the front door - they may be waiting for you! Go to the roof and head down.

You can also leave buildings through windows or by jumping off balconies, if you suspect you'll run into someone - or make too much noise - by using a door.

It's all about playing in weird, surprising ways!

Obviously running through the open can be risky because you're easily seen...

...but it also means you can't easily be ambushed, because there are very few places for anyone to hide!

(And there's also not much reason for anyone else to be there in the first place, since there's hardly any loot out in the open!)

Another advantage of being in the open is it's easier to build some sort of defence if you do come under attack.

Building can sometimes be a problem when you're moving through woods and other more sheltered outdoor areas - the stuff around you can mess up your building at a critical moment.

If you put up a protective wall to fend off an attacker, they'll probably either just keep shooting and break it down, or they'll walk around it and attack you there.

One tactic that can work in this situation is NOT TO HIDE behind your wall. I know this seems like it goes against the whole point of building the wall, but keep on retreating and build another wall behind it - and then keep going, making more walls as you go.

If your opponent keeps advancing, you can sucker them in.

Change tactics just when they don't expect it - maybe wait for them to run out of ammo, and then attack!

Anyway, thanks to Alfie, I seem to be playing solo quite a lot at the moment, which is fine with me - I've been working on my tactics and I've come across a few new things.

I've just worked out how to use a jump pads in a tight spot. If you pick up a jump pad, it'll appear on your building inventory. This is great, as it won't take up space in your main inventory.

A jump pad has to be placed on a full-size built floor, even though it only takes up a quarter of the surface. You can't plant one on a bit of natural ground - so make sure you build a floor first.

To use the jump pad, just run over it.

There are different types of jump pad: one sends the player up in the air, and the other launches them in the direction they were running when they hit the pad.

After using a jump pad, you won't take damage, as long as you land at the same height you took off from.

So be careful about using jump pads from the top of tall structures!

I've also worked out that Solo Fortnite needs a slightly different strategy from playing Duos or Squads.

And who needs to be part of a team when there's so much to do in solo play?

For one thing, you don't have to worry about landing near the rest of your party and you don't have to wait for anyone.

This means you can go down as fast as possible after exiting the Battle Bus!

Your glider auto-deploys before you can get too close to the ground. After it opens you get more than enough time to find your landing spot - in fact if you're not looking out for team mates it can be annoying having to slowly float down when you just want to get on with the match.

You can trick the glider into giving you a quicker landing.

Pick a high spot to land on, but don't aim for it - aim for somewhere nearby that's lower.

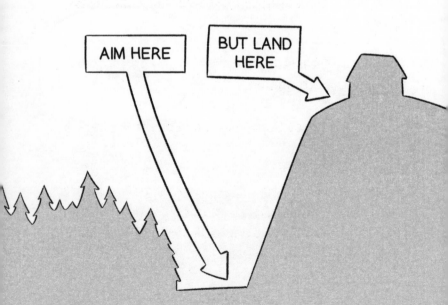

The glider will open later, and you should have enough time to glide from the lower area to the higher one. If you're landing in a popular spot, this tactic could make all the difference.

Don't forget to grab a weapon when you land and be ready to defend yourself.

Another thing to keep in mind when playing in Solo mode is that loot strongholds generally contain more than enough equipment to kit out a whole squad.

So don't get greedy - you won't need it all and there's a limit to how much you can carry.

Just equip yourself as best you can... and then wait.

When the storm starts to close in, you can start to head for the stronghold.

Go in carefully, as there might still be other players hanging around...

Sometimes you'll find that everyone's moved on and that the boss (an NPC) has already been defeated... There's a chance there could be loads of loot just lying around for you to grab!

If you've never defeated this boss yourself, then it's worth taking a look around as you scavenge the loot.

You might pick up a few tips from seeing how it's been done by someone else and knowing the layout will be a big help if you decide to tackle it yourself in another match.

Probably the best thing about playing solo is that you don't have to deal with twitchy, impatient team-mates. You can hide out as long as you're safe from the storm.

Sneaky, stealthy strategies work well when playing solo. Don't rush into battles!

Now all I have to do is sit back and relax.

This is where ambush tactics really work!

Another good thing about solo play is that if you do successfully take out an opponent, you don't have to worry about their teammates hearing the gunfire and coming after you.

And if you see a skirmish happening nearby, you can step in and eliminate the winner.

They'll probably have taken damage in the fight and unlike in Duos or Sqauds, you can be quite sure there won't be any annoying teammates appearing out of nowhere to take revenge on you.

In a squad match there's always a risk of reaching the endgame and finding someone else's entire squad is still in play.

At that point there's a strong chance that the other squad is going to eliminate you and win.

But that's never going to happen in a solo match.

Always keep an eye on the number of remaining players, and when it gets to the last few, don't take any chances.

The storm will close in soon enough and force you all together - so find a good hiding place and let the rest fight each other.

When you're playing solo you won't have anyone like Alfie to help you build a fort in the endgame - so make sure you have enough materials to build up your own.

Picking up materials dropped by eliminated opponents will build your supplies quickly - but be quick to pick it all up, don't let someone target you!

CHAPTER 5

So today we're meant to give a presentation to the rest of the class on our construction project. I checked yesterday with Samson if there was anything he wanted me to do.

"No, nothing at all for you to do," he said. "I've got it all under control."

So I thought: fine, whatever.

Less effort for me.

And then on my way out at the end of the day, Maisie said she needed me to play music at the right moments during her presentation.

"I thought Samson was doing the presentation?" I said.

"Don't be silly," said Maisie. "We agreed this. I'm doing the presentation, just like we discussed."

I should have said something at that point, really - because when I get to school, they're arguing over who's going to give the presentation.

Maisie's spent ages on her design, and she's drawn a comic strip about a tennis match that almost gets rained off, and she's already made it into a PowerPoint presentation.

Samson's made an interactive 3D model of his design, which you can move around and start the conveyor belt running.

Both of them refuse to let the other one give the presentation.

Amy could sort this out.

If she decided which one she wanted to do, the loser wouldn't argue with her.

So it's a shame Amy's not here really!

I don't know where she is, she wanders off sometimes...

Samson tears Maisie's drawing.

Maisie snatches Samson's memory stick, throws it on the floor and stamps on it.

Ms Grimes sends them out of the room. Then she calls on our group.

Someone has to go up and give the presentation... and I'm the only one left...

I haven't prepared anything at all - but there's nothing else for it, I have to go up there.

"Uh..." I begin as the rest of the class stares back at me. "So I thought maybe we might make..."

I look out of the window and see a garage across the street.

"A garage with a door that opens and closes." I turn and draw a garage on the whiteboard.

"And how will you make the door open and close?" asks Ms Grimes.

"Well..." I look at my drawing. "By... opening and closing it."

This is terrible.

As I go on explaining this stupid project I've just made up, I can see the class staring at me like I'm a complete idiot.

I wish I could throw up some walls and take cover until they've all gone...

If only real life was a bit more like Fortnite - when things are going wrong, a simple wall can be a pretty good defence!

A lot of Fortnite players don't really get into building anything more elaborate than a simple wall - and often a few walls and some basic stairs are all you really need to get some quick cover from attacking fire.

But there's a lot more you can do.

Alfie is definitely the best builder I've seen - I've learned quite a few things by watching him.

You might have seen other players like Alfie making structures you didn't even know were possible.

It's worth taking the time to learn how to do some more tricky stuff - and, as with all building in Fortnite, the quicker you can do it, the better, so it's a good idea to pick up a few easy building tips.

For example, here's how to put a window into a wall:

Once you've placed the wall, just choose the edit function. You'll see a grid divided into nine squares.

You can blank out some of the squares to make patterns - this is how you choose how you want to edit the wall.

Blank out the square in the middle and the wall will be rebuilt with a window in the middle. Like this:

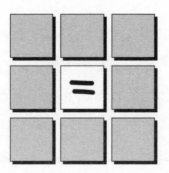

As well as windows and doors, there are lots of other structures you can make by putting different patterns on the grid - it's worth doing some research to get some good ideas.

As soon as the squares on your design turn green, that means you've got a valid pattern and you can make the edit.

I didn't find all the patterns immediately obvious, and it took me a while to get the hang of it.

But once you know which pattern is which - and when you remember the ones you use most - you can edit your walls very quickly, even under pressure in a game situation.

(This is another of those things that's much smoother if you've got a keyboard and mouse, but it can be done with a controller, with a bit of practice.)

Just go into Battle Labs and build something without anyone shooting at you!

In general you can flip any of the basic designs, so if you want a door and window in your wall, but you want them the other way round, just put them the other way around when you make the pattern.

Some structures are definitely more useful than others - arches might look pretty cool but they don't give you much extra cover.

In most cases you're better off just putting a door into your wall - that way, if you need cover you can just close it!

It is worth getting good at building diagonal walls and half walls.

If you include these in your forts, they'll give you good cover to duck behind and much more space to take aim and shoot out of than a smaller window.

The medium and low walls aren't a lot of use on the ground – but they can be a good idea if you make a balcony and don't want to fall off it!

The floor only uses a four-square grid, so there aren't nearly as many edit options and it's much easier to tell which is which.

Of course, you can always choose which way round these structures go - and the edit function will remove any bits of floor you've blanked out on the grid.

If you've put a floor in the wrong place by mistake - like if you've accidentally blocked a staircase - you can quickly edit it and make a gap for the stairs.

But the best use for the floor editing options is making balconies.

Any floor that isn't a full one has a low wall running along its edge, where the shaded part of the grid is.

This makes it much faster and easier to build than to put down a full floor plus a wall along the edge.

This sort of low wall can give you vital cover - you can crouch behind it, then pop up and shoot - and it stops you from falling off!

If you want to add sides to this sort of balcony, you can add them by building a quarter floor on each side.

Or you can make a balcony out of two quarter floors put together.

You can also edit roofs, which use the same four-square grid as the floor.

The basic roof shape is the pyramid, and that'll do for a tower.

But the editing options let you make the shapes you need to build larger sloping roofs that'll fit any structure.

I don't usually bother with fancy roofs in the middle of a Battle Royale - you can just build floors, which will make a flat roof.

If you do decide to use them, the side roof and the outer corner roof are the handiest - you can quickly create a slope with the side roof, or put four outer corners together to make a bigger pyramid.

If you're expecting to get attacked from above, you can also put a floor in underneath your roof - this will give you some extra warning if someone starts breaking in.

Editing stairs is slightly different, because you're not just dealing with the shape - you also need to decide on the direction of the stairs.

Instead of just clicking on each part of the grid, you need to swoosh the cursor round it to change the direction of the arrows.

This takes a bit of practice so you can always try it out in Battle Labs where you have more time to play around without fear of being shot by an opponent!

If you do have time on your hands, then a bit of editing can really give your fort the edge.

Or you can do what Alfie and I used to do - assign one squad member to do the building while the others look out for attacks!

You're probably wondering by now - how much of this sort of complicated building is worth doing, if you're in the middle of a match?

Because let's be honest, this isn't Minecraft and we don't all have Alfie's anti-shooting qualms!

When you're playing Fortnite you're not going to get much time to enjoy a really well-made building.

One way or the other, the match will be over and it'll be gone.

If you don't really like building, look out for a Port-a-Fort - it's an instant tower that springs up on the spot where you throw it.

A Port-a-Fort can really save the day in certain situations, but it does take up an inventory slot that you could use for weapons... Is it worth using up a slot?

Well, yes - if you're a sneakier player, who rarely uses weapons until the endgame, it's totally worth it - and it can give you the edge over players who are better at building.

Alfie! Look upon my Port-a-Fort and TREMBLE!

CHAPTER 6

I'm getting ready for school one morning when I'm surprised to see Mum standing by the door with a suitcase. I ask her where she's going.

"Honestly," she says, rolling her eyes. "I knew you weren't listening when I told you about this."

"I was," I say, trying to remember the last time she told me something.

"You had your head in your game again."

OK, this is her fault. I have told her not to tell me important things when I'm in the middle of a match!

A taxi pulls up outside our house.

"Dad will explain - I've got to go." She shouts "Bye!" to Dad, wherever he is, and carries her suitcase through the front door.

I walk into the kitchen and Dad hands me a plate of toast without looking up.

"Thanks," I say.

Dad looks up. "I thought you were Mum."

"No, she just left."

Dad looks around, confused. "She didn't say anything."

"She did, you weren't listening. So where did she go?"

"She's going on an away day."

Between the two of us, we *nearly* know what's going on around here!

"What's an away day?"

"It's when you go somewhere with people from work, and do something different from normal work. Sometimes they're fun - I once did one where we had paintballing."

"What's paintballing?"

"Actually," says Dad as he plucks his toast from the toaster and starts to butter it, "it's a lot like that game you're into."

"Fortnite?"

"Yeah. Except you do it in real life."

I find it hard to believe Dad's boss dropped everyone he works with onto an island and made them all fight to the death, and I tell him this.

"Oh you don't use real guns, obviously – they've got little balls of paint in them, and if you get splatted with the paint, you know you've been hit."

"Cool. So did you hit anyone?"

Dad smiles as he sits down with his toast.

"I splatted Mark from Accounts when he was hiding in a hollow and thought no-one could see him. I ambushed Jenny from Sales when she was busy trying to hit the work experience kid. I took down three of the Customer Services team while they were arguing over which way to go..."

He's loving telling me about all this, and I'm starting to think Dad might be...

... quite good at Fortnite?

He's telling me his plans for this evening while Mum's away (pizzas on the sofa, watching his old comedy DVDs) but I'm distracted...

I can't help wondering what it would be like if Dad did play Fortnite...

Refusing to revive you after you get knocked down unless you say "please" and "thank you"...

Telling you not to drink all your shield potions at once because you might be thirsty later...

"What's so funny?" asks Dad.

"Oh nothing," I say, "So, what's the point of these away days? Apart from them just being fun and stuff?"

"They call it team building," says Dad. "It's supposed to let you all get to know each other more, so you work together better, and it teaches you how to co-operate. And all that sort of thing."

I'm starting to get an idea. "Does it work?"

"Oh yeah, once you've teamed up with a colleague to take down someone else who annoys you, you've always got that bond."

He glances at the clock on the microwave. "Aren't you going to be late for school?"

He's right, I am - and I haven't packed my bag yet either.

"You should do it the night before," Dad says, going back to his sudoku. "You're so disorganised. I've no idea how you manage to find so much time for that game you play."

Hmm... Maybe there's something in what he says...

Lots of Fortnite players are totally chaotic, but there's value in being organised.

Instead of leaving your inventory in the order it falls, you can use the inventory view to rearrange your items. On a keyboard you open inventory view by pressing 'I', and on a console you press up on the D-pad.

As well as being able to highlight items and swap them into different slots, you can drop them altogether if you want to give them to a teammate - and you can also drop materials and ammo.

You can also check out the specs of each weapon you're carrying!

This is great if, like me, you sometimes get confused over which type of SMG is better for what, or you want to compare weapons of different types and classes (say, if you only have space for one more gun and can't decide between a rare pistol or an uncommon charge shotgun).

If you get a spare moment, take some time to get organised.

Different players have different views on what order you should keep your inventory in, and a lot of them will argue about it for hours and hours.

Most players agree that it makes sense to keep all your guns together so you can switch between them easily in a combat situation, and don't have to skip past a medkit on your way to your shotgun.

Remember when I talked about switching between weapons when they're out of ammo? It makes sense.

So I like to fill up my slots from the left with all my guns - then I use my next free slot for explosives, if I have any.

The slot on the far right can be used for healing items - again, if I'm carrying more than one healing item, I always keep them together!

Now, you could organise your guns by what class they're in - so if you've got a rare weapon, an uncommon one and a common one, put them in that order.

The advantage of that is that if you find a better weapon, you know where your weakest one is and can swap it very quickly - and you can instantly move to your strongest weapon in combat!

But in combat, you should use the most appropriate weapon rather than the best one - which is why I think the best way to organise your weapons is by range.

Let's say you've got a shotgun, an assault rifle, a sniper rifle and an SMG.

I'd arrange them in this order:

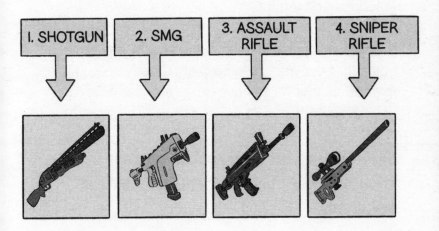

| 1. SHOTGUN | 2. SMG | 3. ASSAULT RIFLE | 4. SNIPER RIFLE |

You might start off using the SMG, and then run out of ammo or need to reload - in which case you'll want to swap to your next best weapon at that range, the assault rifle.

Weapons that work in similar combat situations are best kept next to each other, because they're the ones you're likely to need at the same time.

And of course, if you're going to go for the double-weapon technique, like carrying two shotguns, you should put them next to each other in your inventory!

Find whatever inventory arrangement works best for you - and of course, it all depends on what weapons you find in a match.

If you have explosives and a sniper rifle, for instance, you might not want to keep them together - you might find it better to have the explosives next to your assault rifle.

But if you use the same system for your inventory every time you play, you'll have an advantage.

Switching between your weapons can become automatic and you won't need to think about where each item is - you'll know your SMG will be next to your assault rifle, and can switch to it instantly.

You can go one step further with this, depending on how you play the game - if you're the kind of player who grabs the first weapon they find and rushes into combat, then you'll have to fight with whatever you get.

But if, like me, you try to go through quieter areas, and rifle through a few chests before you get near any other players, you're more likely to have a choice of weapons - and you can hang onto your favourites.

So I'm going to take Dad's advice for once and get organised.

My plan is to keep a similar inventory in every match I play - and then I can put the same weapons in the same slots so I know exacty where everything is!

Players who use keyboards tend to use this method, because unlike console gamers they don't have to shuttle left and right across their inventory.

They can bind certain keys to certain weapons and switch to the weapon they need with the twitch of a finger. This can be a big advantage in a match - if a certain key is always your shotgun, you can draw it

without a second thought. If you usually play on a console, but have access to a PC that can run Fortnite, it's worth trying out.

In fact, maybe I can use Mum's laptop while she's away...

CHAPTER 7

So this is the state of our construction project at the moment:

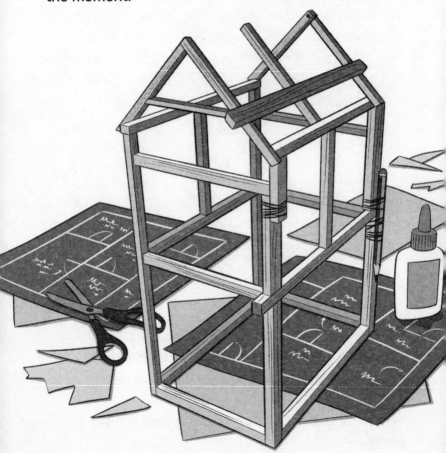

Yeah, I know.

We still haven't really settled on what to make... or how to make it... or what to make it from.

But apart from that it's going great.

We've made a sort of frame thing out of wood that could be made into Maisie's design or Samson's design, and it's obvious they're each hoping the other will give in, or maybe go off sick and the other one will get a chance to grab control of the project.

This is why we need my brilliant new idea.

(Well, I hate to say it, but it's not all my idea as it's totally based on that conversation I had with Dad about getting organised and shooting people you have to work with!)

"I've had a brilliant new idea," I say.

Maisie and Samson are arguing over whether a strip of fabric she's brought in should be used as a tennis net or a conveyor belt, and Amy's watching videos of shark attacks on her phone.

None of them have heard me, so I say it again.

"Everyone, I've had a brilliant new idea!"

"Really?" says Maisie: she doesn't sound very convinced.

"Alright, fine," says Samson. "What is it?"

"I think after school today we should all get together and play some Fortnite."

Maisie's not impressed. "I thought you meant an idea about the project, Tyler? You know, the thing we're meant to be doing?"

"Yeah, I know we're meant to be doing it," I say, "and we're not getting very far, are we?"

"How will it help if we play computer games?" says Samson.

"It's called a team-building exercise. Companies do them when they want to -"

Samson shakes his head quickly. "Yeah OK, very interesting, but I don't do those kind of games, Tyler."

Amy looks up. "You should try them. They're really good."

"I can see someone like *you*'d enjoy them, but I don't get anything out of them at all."

"Huh. You must be doing them wrong," says Amy, and goes back to her phone.

Samson keeps arguing with Amy, but she's lost interest in talking to him.

Then I have another thought, one which might save my brilliant idea.

"What do you say, Maisie?" I ask. "We could play a couple of matches and in between we could talk about the project."

I can see Maisie's thinking about what she can get out of this.

She and Samson have both given up trying to get Amy to support their idea - she doesn't care enough to take a side - which means if I get behind one of them, the other will be outvoted.

(Thing is, I don't want to pick one and annoy the other... and I like both ideas about the same anyway.)

"Why not?" says Maisie, smiling. "OK."

"But you hate Fortnite!" says Samson.

"Who said I hate Fortnite?"

"You did, last week!"

Maisie shrugs. "Just because you refuse ever to change your mind about anything ever, doesn't mean the rest of us can't."

"But you can't do it if the rest of us aren't doing it, that's not fair."

"You can't stop us. Amy – are you in?"

"Yeah, I suppose," says Amy. "I'll probably be playing tonight anyway..."

Samson looks at Amy, Maisie and me in turn, furious at the idea he might be left out.

"Fine," he says grumpily. "I'll play too."

"Great!" I tell them, and explain what Samson and Maisie need to do to install the game. We arrange to play later that evening once Samson and Maisie have finished their homework (and when Amy has finished, uh, whatever it is that she does).

Once we're all agreed and they know what to do, I look at my phone and realise Amy has already sent me a friend request.

Amy... a friend?

It doesn't sound right.

But anyway, the important thing is I got them all to agree. It looks like the match is on!

CHAPTER 8

It's late afternoon, I'm home from school, and we're nearly ready to get started.

Alfie's on the sofa - he just came over and I said I was busy with a Fortnite match, and he said he didn't mind just watching.

"I do sort of need to concentrate," I told him, and explained all about my team bonding idea.

He said it was fine, and that I wouldn't even notice he was here, and went to get himself a Coke Zero from the fridge.

I can definitely notice he's here. He makes a lot of noise when he drinks out of a can.

I've got my new headphones and mic ready, but I'm beginning to have a few second thoughts about my brilliant idea....

Alfie has helpfully just pointed out that good squad play is one of the trickier things to learn in Fortnite, because it depends on who you're playing with - not exactly the dream team in my case.

But I tell him that squad play is also one of the most impressive things in the game – we've all seen those awesome squads who ruthlessly sweep through matches and don't give anyone else a chance.

Okay, so that's not likely to be my squad today and I can't tell you how to be on one of those squads. I wish I could!

But I do know a few ways you can improve your squad play.

First of all, think about whether Squad mode is right for you? Different Fortnite modes suit different players.

If you're a really reckless player, Squads probably isn't your thing. Play Solo, or maybe Duos with a like-minded friend.

That way, if you take risks and get eliminated early, it doesn't matter to anyone else - you can load up another match and go again.

If you bomb out of a Squads match, you're putting the rest of your team at a disadvantage.

Your team will have to stop and heal you, or use your reboot card, or they'll have to go on without you.

Of course, you can keep playing a Squads match if you've lost team members, but it's going to be really tough to win if you're up against another squad which stays together until the endgame.

Try not to make it even harder for your teammates by leaving them one person short in the endgame!

If you're someone who wants to follow your own strategy, but you enjoy the challenge of going up against other teams all on your own, then you can always play Squads on 'Don't Fill'.

This is an option where you play as a squad but choose not to fill the last three slots of the four.

That way you won't put three other random players at a disadvantage by making them play with a team of three.

Bring it on!

(This is exactly the kind of thing I can imagine Ellie doing before she partnered up with Alfie. And I wouldn't be suprised if it's the way Amy plays as well.)

If you're serious about playing as a squad, and maximising your chances as a team, then the first thing you need to agree on is where you're going to land.

When I'm playing solo, I always try to avoid landing between a loot stronghold and the centre of the map. Other players who land at the stronghold will pick up what they need and head for the centre and you don't want to run into them - fully armed - on your way!

But Alfie reminds me that my landing tactics might be different if I'm working as a squad with enough firepower to take out any opponents we might meet early on.

And if I make a last-minute decision and bail out, the rest of my squad will be scrambling to catch up.

Whatever Alfie says, I reckon it's a general rule that hitting the ground first can put you at a big advantage, so make sure everyone has time to consider the best moment to bail out of the bus and where to aim.

And yes Alfie, I will consider the rest of the team when I pick a spot!

I'm probably going to be at ease dropping into somewhere that's going to be really busy, because I'm pretty quick at finding weapons and going on the attack – but I'm guessing the others on my squad won't be quite so clever.

So I'm planning to share out any items I don't need and make sure everyone has some sort of weapon and some healing items to start off with - hopefully I'll be able to find enough to go around.

This isn't about being generous - it's about survival!

If my teammates don't have anything to fight with or heal themselves, they're likely to be eliminated early - and that's bad for me too.

Alfie reminds me that sometimes a teammate who seems a bit hopeless and doesn't even know which item is which, might end up being the one who grabs your reboot card and keeps you in the match.

Anyway, I'm thinking it's probably best to split up at the start of the match so that we can search the immediate area for loot.

I'll make sure we all keep in touch and I'll let the others know if I've found two of the same weapon, or two with similar range.

I won't just leave a shotgun lying around because I've already got one - someone else on my team could use it!

I'll either take it with me or, if my inventory's full, I'll make a note of where it is and tell the other guys they can come and get it.

Okay - I've got this - and finally everyone has joined.

I'm ready to explain to Samson and Maisie how to play, and to outline the game plan for our first match.

Maisie's already read up on it a bit, and she starts telling me stuff I already know. I try to get her to stop it so we can start the match.

I was hoping Amy might be able to help me out with this bit, but she's got bored and gone off to make herself a sandwich.

Amy 81xp

(And then I notice Amy's got a pretty cool looking avatar and an XP of 81!)

I didn't even know she played, but she must play quite a lot as that is pretty impressive - maybe bigger than anyone else I've played with from school!

"Cool skin, Amy," I say – and I mean it, I'm pretty jealous.

"Yeah, cheers, whatever," comes Amy's voice over the chat.

I've never got round to updating from the noob skin, as I've always been obsessed with tactics and getting to Victory Royale, but this gets me thinking maybe it would be cool to try out a new Fortnite skin...

But before I have time to think about this properly, Samson interrupts with a long list of VERY SPECIFIC questions.

He seems to be taking this Fortnite thing about as seriously as he takes his schoolwork, and is shooting a volley of questions through the chat like machine gun fire!

I actually know the last one, and I'm about to answer when Amy speaks again:

"Five seconds for wood, twelve seconds for brick, twenty seconds for metal. Can we just get on with the match?"

"I agree," I say, "you'll get to grips with it much quicker if we actually play, so –"

"Hang on a minute!" says Maisie.

"What's the matter?"

"I'm still choosing my outfit."

Of *course* she is.

When we first lined up on the platform, Maisie had been given the same default noob skin as me.

"You still use the noob skins?" says Alfie from the sofa.

"Yeah, so what?" I reply.

"Just thought that, since you spend so much time playing Fortnite, you might get a Battle Pass or something."

"'It doesn't make you play better. It's a waste of money."

"But it's more fun when you earn new stuff each time you level up."

I'm starting to get a little bit sick of the fact that Alfie seems to be the resident expert on everything to do with Fortnite, even though if it wasn't for me he'd never even have played it.

And he wouldn't have met Ellie or any of my school friends either.

"I thought I wouldn't even know you were here?"

"Sorry..."

So anyway, Maisie has splashed out for some V-bucks and got herself a new look.

"Uh... Maisie..." I say, "that's cool and everything, but you might want to find out if you like the game first?"

"I'm not going to go into a Fortnite match looking like everyone else," says Maisie, "and certainly not looking like *you*."

"Can. We. Just. Play?" says Amy, and I can see her eyes rolling and hear her teeth gritting from here.

I don't blame her.

I'm losing patience with this too.

"Yeah, come on," I say and launch the match. Here we go!

The moment we enter the lobby, Samson and Maisie pick up guns and start shooting each other.

"You can't kill people in the lobby," I say.

"I know that," says Samson. "Just practising."

"And you can't kill your own squad members in the proper game either."

"Oh, what? Why not?"

"Because that's not the point of the game!"

"Look," I say, "when the match starts, follow my lead, go where I go and stick together, right?"

"Right," say Maisie and Samson reluctantly.

"Amy?" I say. "Is, er, that OK with you?"

Amy doesn't say anything – but then, that's pretty normal for her.

"Amy?" I try again.

"Yeah, whatever," she replies. "I don't play Squads much, I always do Solo matches."

I find this very easy to believe.

When Amy does play Squads I bet she's one of those players - a bit like Ellie - who lands in a totally different place to the rest of the squad and follows their own strategy.

Chances are we won't see Amy again until she turns up in the endgame with all the best weapons.

But for now, she seems willing to stick together, so maybe this team-building idea is going to work after all...

"This map is useless," Samson complains, "it's all covered in question marks."

"That's because you're new at the game," I tell him. "You have to explore everywhere before you get the map."

"That's not very fair," says Maisie. "Can't you pay to get the full map?"

"No you can't," I say. "You have to explore it yourself."

"Can you buy better weapons?"

"No. You can only pay for outfits and stuff to jazz up your avatar."

"So... you can only buy stuff that doesn't help you win the game?"

"Yes."

The battle bus is launching, but Maisie hasn't finished complaining...

"That's *silly*," she says. "They could make so much money if they let you buy all the best weapons! The people who make this game don't know what they're doing."

"It means," says Amy, "you can't buy your way to a Victory Royale. You have to get good at the game if you want to win it. So it's fair."

I think this is the most I've ever heard Amy speak. Even more surprising is the fact I agree with her.

"Yeah... well said, Amy," I say.

"Everybody out," she replies.

I realise too late that the bus has reached the end. We're being booted out!

I got completely distracted by all the arguing, and we don't even have a plan!

CHAPTER 9

OK, so my team is falling through the sky, and I have zero idea what we're going to do next.

"We're all following you," says Samson in a slightly aggro way. "So where are we going?"

"I think you should go there," says Alfie, walking right up to the TV and tapping part of the map.

"Outta the way!" I snap at him.

"Sorry," he shrugs and goes back to the sofa.

Annoyingly he's right, it is the best option. It's not a great spot for loot, especially since we'll have to share it between four of us, but it'll be quiet.

I move the cursor to the sticky fingerprint Alfie has left on the screen, put a marker on it, then dive down.

Amy and I land on the roof and find two weapons - we grab one each.

The others will have to wait until we find something else, which they won't like but it's silly to give the only guns to people who can't use them.

Amy gets on with bashing through the roof to the room below, which seems a good job for her to do.

I'm just thinking that as soon as Maisie and Samson land, we should probably all jump down there and -

Hang on. Where are Maisie and Samson?

I can't see them anywhere.

"Amy's with me, where are the rest of you?" I ask.

"Still in the sky," says Maisie. "Why didn't you tell me how you do that thing to make you fall faster?"

I forgot to tell them about that. I remembered to tell them about thanking the bus driver, but I forgot to tell them that!

But isn't it obvious?

"You push up on the thumbstick," I say.

"You push up to go down?"

"Yes."

"That's stupid."

"Actually it's not," says Samson, "it's called inverting the Y-axis, it's the same principle that aeroplane controls use –"

"Alright, if you're so clever, what are you doing still

floating around up here with me?"

"It said on the screen to press X to open the glider, so I pressed X to open the glider."

"Look," I say, "can you two just hurry up and get down here so we can get some cover - "

And then someone shoots me in the back, and I've got other worries.

See, this is exactly why you get inside a building *fast* after you land!

I've got to react quickly if I'm not going to get eliminated in the first few seconds - that'll ruin the whole team-bonding thing - so I turn quickly and switch to my weapon -

And there's no-one there.

But on the roof of the next building along are a load of items, just scattered around.

I realise that whoever was shooting at me, they were on that other rooftop - and someone else has eliminated them.

Next to me Amy is reloading the sniper rifle she picked up after we landed.

Wow. She took them out with one shot!

"Er... thanks," I say.

"We need to get inside," she says. "Can't wait around for those two, the rest of their squad might be near and you need a medkit."

And with that she jumps into the hole she's made in our roof, and I follow her.

The room we drop into has got a chest in it, and Amy tells me to search it while she bashes down to the next floor.

"Usually I'd tell a team-mate to land on the other roof, grab that loot and search that building, then meet us here," Amy says. "But it's too risky, they don't know what they're doing."

"We can hear you, you know," says Samson.

"I know,'" says Amy.

Finally the others land and the team is assembled - and I've found a medkit and healed myself.

Amy stands at the window with her sniper rifle and watches out for the teammates of that player she eliminated.

"Don't like it," she says. "They must be around somewhere..."

Unfortunately we've hit a problem: we've found enough weapons for everyone to have at least one to start off with, including two pistols which are the best guns for our two noobs to use... but one of the pistols is common, while the other is uncommon.

This really isn't a big deal, right?

Wrong.

"I don't see why she should get the better pistol," says Samson.

"Because green is my lucky colour," says Maisie.

"There's no such thing as luck!"

"And I don't like grey."

"I don't think green is your lucky colour at all - I think you're making this up so you can have a better gun than me."

"There's hardly any difference," I tell them. "We'll find better guns in a minute anyway when we move on somewhere else."

"What if we don't?" says Maisie.

"We will."

"But what if we don't?"

Then Amy returns to the building (I hadn't noticed she'd left) and throws down two blue shotguns in front of Samson and Maisie.

She must have just gone out and somehow got them from outside.

Huh. I didn't even notice.

Samson picks both of them up. "Thanks," he says. "You can have the green pistol, Maisie."

"Hey!" says Maisie.

"It's all quiet out there," says Amy. "Let's make a move."

"Let Maisie have one of the shotguns," I tell Samson.

I'm starting to feel strangely like how I imagined Dad would be in Fortnite!

"Fine," Samson says. "Which is better, charge shotgun or tactical shotgun?"

"I'm not telling you. Just give one of them to Maisie."

There's a pause while Samson compares the specs.

This is getting really annoying.

"Hurry up, the storm's closing in! We need to get out of here."

He drops the charge shotgun, after I explain to him how you use the inventory view to drop things.

Finally, we move on.

Back in my living room, Alfie laughs. "This is fun."

For some people, maybe!

I'm beginning to HATE my brilliant idea.

I think I'd even rather be on a squad with Leon than this lot!

Before long we come to the next building and someone starts shooting at us - probably the teammates of the player Amy shot on the roof.

"Zig-zag!" I shout and start running towards the building in a zig-zag pattern.

"What?" says Samson as he's shot and falls down.

"Maisie, revive him."

"Why do I have to do it?" she says. "It's his fault he got shot."

I'm beginning to get a little bit irritated now. And Alfie's not helping.

He's enjoying this far too much.

"Because Amy and I are busy trying to shoot the people who shot him so they don't shoot you!" I snap.

"Hurry up, Maisie! I'm going to die in a minute!" Samson wails.

So far this is not working out quite like I planned.

Meanwhile Amy has got a firefly from somewhere and has set fire to the house our opponents are shooting at us from, which has given them something else to think about for the moment.

"Watch the front, Tyler," she says, and I understand what she's planning - I wait by the front door while she runs round the back.

I hear gunfire as she eliminates two of them.

The other runs out the front door and I get him - weakened by the fire, he's easy enough to take down.

Among his dropped loot are two medkits, which I take back to Samson.

We heal Samson and prepare to move on... but -

"Where's Maisie?" I ask.

"I found loads of stuff!" she replies over the chat.

I look up at the map to see where she is - by a bend in the river.

"What are you doing over there?" says Amy.

"Picking up awesome loot," says Maisie. "Hey, what's that annoying music?"

You should never go there. There's a bunch of tough NPCs who hang around there.

"Maisie, get out of there!" I say. "There's a bunch of NPCs coming your way!"

"What are NPCs?" she says.

A rattle of gunfire comes from her direction.

"Maisie," I say, "just come back - quick!"

"Alright, there's no need to shout," says Maisie as she starts running our way.

"I think we should start running too," says Amy.

"Ellie always says not to split the party," says Alfie.

"We wait for Maisie!" I tell the rest of my squad.

"Yeah, but she's leading those NPCs straight to us," says Amy, and she's got a point.

"I'm getting out of here," says Samson.

"Wait!" I say - but he's already running.

Maisie heads our way, bullets spraying across the field.

"Give her some covering fire!" I shout.

"Do we have to?"Amy replies.

"Yes - come on, we're not leaving anyone behind."

This isn't much of a team bonding exercise if we abandon each other to die, is it?

Plus, I'm worried that if Maisie or Samson get eliminated they won't want to hang around watching

HELP ME!!

Amy and me play, no matter how awesome we are, and they'll go off and do something else.

So we raise our weapons – a sniper rifle for Amy and an assault rifle for me – and take aim at the NPCs chasing Maisie...

But before either of us can get a shot away, Maisie falls.

She's been eliminated!

"Now we have to leave her," says Amy.

"I'll get her reboot card," I say.

Amy sighs. "You're gonna say you want me to cover you, aren't you..."

I start running!

In some ways it's good Maisie's been eliminated rather than just knocked down – if I had to stand in the middle of the battlefield healing her, I'd be a sitting target.

Those NPCs are still heading our way – so I need to be quick!

"Samson?" I yell. "Are you near a reboot van?"

"What's a reboot van?" he replies.

"Look on the map - those blue circles, like the off button on a TV remote. You need to get to one of those to use Maisie's reboot card."

"I haven't got Maisie's reboot card."

"I'm just about to get it for you!"

I pick up the card and start running back, zigzagging to avoid the NPCs' bullets.

"Right," I tell Samson. "Go to the van and use the card."

"Um... yep, will do. But it might take me a while."

"Why?"

"I got knocked down again and I'm doing that thing where you crawl around."

"Again?!"

"'Yeah."

"You can't use the reboot card while you're knocked down!"

"Oh right. Can someone come and get me up then? Oh no - actually don't worry, I think I'm dead again now."

"So who's going to reboot me now?" complains Maisie.

"I don't know," I say, "I've –"

All this talking has distracted me and I've forgotten to keep zigzagging. One of the NPCs has taken me out with a clean headshot.

"Stuff this," says Amy, spraying the NPCs with her SMG. She takes two of them down, but the third gets her.

We have placed #19.

"Well that was great," says Samson without sounding at all like he means it, "I guess I'll see you all tomorrow."

"No!" I say. "Come on everyone! Let's go for another match – you'll play much better now you know what you're doing."

The next match we play, Maisie mistakes us for enemy players and chucks a grenade at us.

The noise attracts another squad, who turn up and eliminate us all while we're still recovering.

We try again, but this time Samson insists on stopping to take down a shark, and we get ambushed while we're trying to convince him to move on.

Then the shark kills him.

CHAPTER 10

So, things aren't working out exactly how I'd planned, but I'm not prepared to give up on my brilliant idea just yet!

"I'm not sure if it's technically possible, but I think they're actually getting worse," says Alfie.

"I know," I reply.

I'm waiting for the next match to load and wondering whether anyone else would like to point out how badly this is going, when I get a text from from Amy.

They're actually getting worse

I text back:

Yes I know

But amazingly, this next match seems to be going OK so far. Somehow we make Survivor II, and then get into a clearing at the centre of the storm circle, and I start to explain all about building in Fortnite.

This is a mistake.

Maisie and Samson immediately start making separate forts.

I try to tell them we should be working together, making one fort we can all use - but they completely ignore me and keep building higher and higher.

"It's not a competition to see who can build the biggest fort," I say as they go on competing with each other to build the biggest fort.

They both ignore me.

"It was pretty obvious this was going to happen," says Amy.

She's right. I should have seen this coming a mile away.

Of course they're not pulling together. They're acting exactly like they do in real life!

It's SO frustrating!

Samson falls off his tower and dies, and Amy and I are so busy laughing at him we let another squad sneak up on us and take us both out.

Then they hack the base of Maisie's tower to pieces so it collapses, and she hits the ground hard too.

Samson's about to storm off because we laughed at him, and I don't want this to make everything worse, so we apologise (well, I apologise) and we go into another match.

This is it. I'm absolutely determined this will be the one where we work together and it all goes right and we get that Victory Royale and it becomes a brilliant experience that proves we can be a great team!

We make a good start - we find an isolated spot and get some lucky strikes with our first few chests.

We're nice and tooled up, and Amy's found a helicopter.

"Ellie and I don't use helicopters," says Alfie, and I just ignore him.

It's not like everyone has to play like him and Ellie.
I've got my *own* way.

Amy's at the controls as we take off...

"This is cool!" says Samson.

"Yeah," says Maisie, "it's like getting the VIP treatment!"

Wow! They actually agreed on something!

But it can't possibly last, and it doesn't. Samson thinks we should head straight for the centre of the map and camp out there.

I try to explain to him why that might not be the wisest strategy.

Maisie, meanwhile, is determined we should keep the helicopter as long as we can, because she likes it, and she shouts both of us down if we suggest landing anywhere at all.

If this is going to work, I'm just going to have to make a decision and put my foot down.

"We should go to that small island," I say firmly.

Samson and Maisie go on arguing.

But who cares?

Amy will listen to me.

"Amy, take us to that island please," I say, putting a marker on the map.

Amy doesn't reply.

For a moment I think she just can't hear me over all the other shouting in the group chat.

"Amy?" I say.

Amy still doesn't reply.

"Um, I think she's left the match," says Alfie.

"Shut up, Alfie!" I say - but then I realise he's right.

The pilot seat is empty.

Amy's gone!

We're heading for a mountain!

AND NO-ONE IS FLYING THE HELICOPTER!

After we've all crashed and died, we agree that's a good place to end the session and log out.

There's not much point going on now that Amy has disappeared.

"Wow," says Alfie. "That didn't go well."

"No thanks to you," I reply.

"What did I do?"

"You just sat there making annoying comments, putting me off –"

"I was trying to help! Ellie and I play a lot, and –"

"I'm sick of hearing about Ellie and you! I'm not Ellie! Or you! And I'm not taking Fortnite tips from someone who's never made an elimination!"

"That's not true – I've made two by mistake!"

"Why don't you just shut up and leave me alone!"

And he does.

After he's gone, I think about what went wrong.

Because Alfie is right - that did not go well at all. It's no wonder we got nowhere in any of those matches.

Arguing over decisions in Fortnite wastes time and is distracting.

But maybe my team-building wasn't a total failure after all - at least I now know that if you can't make collective decisions quickly, and if no one will take turns to be in charge, then you need a good team leader who can make the final decision.

And next time, that team leader is NOT going to be me!

CHAPTER 11

I need someone to moan to. Usually I'd moan to Alfie, but he's one of the people I want to moan *about*.

I stick my Switch in a bag and walk, wondering where to go... and I end up at Sana's house.

Feels a bit weird to just drop in on her, but I'm here now...

I ring the bell.

Through the door I hear Sana shout to her older brother, "Can you get that? I'm in the middle of a match!"

"So am I!" her brother shouts back.

I wait on the doorstep for a few minutes and eventually her brother gets eliminated from his match and comes to the door.

"Who are you?" he asks.

I start telling him I'm a friend of Sana's, but he loses interest halfway through the sentence and goes back to the living room.

"Er, it's me, Tyler!" I shout up to Sana.

She says I can come up if I bring some biscuits from her kitchen. Which is fair enough - they live in a tall house and her bedroom is at the top.

When I arrive with the biscuits, Sana finishes a

match (she's placed #4) and breaks off from playing while she eats.

That's a real pro tip right there:

Don't try to play Fortnite and eat at the same time!

"So what's happening?" she says, a little bit suspiciously - obviously wondering why I'm here.

"Oh," I say, shrugging, "I had a stupid idea and it went really badly."

She smiles. "Yeah, that can happen with stupid ideas."

"I think that's where I went wrong. I should've had a *good* idea instead."

"What was your stupid idea then?"

"'Playing Fortnite with my design project group."

She laughs. "Oh, I wish you'd told me! I'd have loved to spectate that match."

I actually recorded some of it on my Switch, so I get it out and show her.

"So, do you want to have a proper match where you're not playing with idiots?" she asks.

"I'd *love* to have a proper match where I'm not playing with idiots."

We go for a Duos match and play it nice and relaxed, moving inwards from the edge of the map.

"So how's your group going with the project?" I ask while we're waiting to see what the storm's going to do next.

"Don't ask," she groans. "You know Leon did the presentation for our group because I was at my music lesson?"

I tell her don't actually remember what Leon said at the presentation, because I was distracted by all the problems in my group.

"He took the credit for everything!" Sana says. "He made it all sound like it was his idea!"

"Typical Leon. Whose idea was it?"

"Mostly mine. He actually seems to think it's true, though. He's the kind of person who just repeats your idea back to you and thinks it was his all along, you know? He doesn't even understand how the mechanism in ours works!"

"It'd be funny if he claimed all the credit, then it didn't work and you had to fix it."

"Haha! Yeah, that would be hilarious... Hey, great shot."

I've just used my assault rifle to knock down someone on a hilltop.

"Yeah, I've been practising using the assault rifle at range," I say.

(In fact it's something I've seen her do and wanted to copy, but I don't tell her that.)

"It's why the assault rifle's the best weapon," she says as we move in closer to take the opponent out. "I always carry one, even if all I can find is a common."

"Anyway, at least your group's got an idea," I say, reluctantly moving the conversation away from my awesome elimination. "My group's got nothing. That's why I did the team-bonding thing."

And so we go on moaning – she tells me about how Leon talks over her all the time, I tell her about how Samson and Maisie are determined to do their idea and how Amy keeps going AWOL.

"Although actually, she was the best at Fortnite by miles," I say. "She had really good strategy. I think she's cleverer than she lets on."

By this time, I'm not really thinking about how well we're doing - I'm not even checking the counter of how many players are left.

We win a firefight with another duo, but Sana's knocked down, so I heal her and then quickly look around - surely someone's going to attack us any moment?

Suddenly these words rush up onto the screen:

VICTORY ROYALE

"Huh," says Sana. "I didn't even notice we were winning."

"Me neither." Someone else must've got caught in the storm or run into an NPC. "I think we won by accident."

"They all count!" says Sana.

If only I could have been in the same group as Sana for the design project - we make a great team. We'd have aced it!

But I guess that's life - Mum and Dad are always moaning about people they work with.

On the way home, I'm still thinking about how hard it is to play with a squad.

Playing Duos with Sana was so easy compared to yesterday's fiasco! And when you're playing Solo you only have to please yourself.

But with Squads, there are so many tough decisions to make and no matter how hard you try, you won't always be able to keep everyone happy.

For instance, sometimes you have to decide when it's worth keeping your teammates in the match and when to leave them behind.

If the storm's closing in and healing your teammate will mean going into it, don't do it - or not unless you can get back out of the storm quickly!

If you're in a tricky situation, it can actually be better if your teammate needs rebooting rather than healing.

Once you've picked up the reboot card, there's no time limit on being able to use it, and the player will revive with full health, though obviously their weapons will be rubbish.

If you don't have much in the way of healing items, or if your teammate's inventory isn't that great (say, if they've been knocked down very early), you might be better off letting them get eliminated - especially if you're under attack.

Don't take too many risks - you're no good to your teammates if you're dead too!

If the opposition are still around, your priority should be to get rid of the danger.

This is kind of obvious if they're shooting at you and there's no-one else to shoot back!

But it can be tempting to leave your other teammates to fight while you do the healing, and then return to the fray.

Thing is, in the meantime this will leave your squad even more outnumbered – if there were four of you before, suddenly there's only two.

So keep firing on the enemy – if you defeat them, there'll be time to heal later.

If you're a quick builder, throw up a wall to give a fallen teammate something to hide behind - but don't take your eyes off the enemy!

If you've got a designated builder on your team, this is where they can come in useful.

(Thinking back, most of my previous successes in Squads were at least partly down to Alfie - he was always picking up materials in the background, and was on hand to quickly throw up a structure whenever we could use one.)

A wall - or even better, a small hut - will not only protect your teammate, it'll also protect any teammate who goes to revive them.

This could be really important if another squad is watching your battle, waiting to step in and eliminate the winners...

You're never more vulnerable to a sniper shot than when you've just been in battle and you're healing a fallen teammate.

This can leave you even more exposed than when you're picking up someone's loot, as you're probably not at full health from the battle.

Your teammate is probably lying out in the open, and healing means standing still for several seconds.

It's the perfect opportunity for the enemy!

So you can either put up some walls to protect yourself, or carry your teammate to a safe spot before healing.

If you don't have time, get another squad member - ideally someone like Alfie - to put some walls up for you.

If you're the one who's been knocked down and your teammates are still fighting, it may seem sensible to crawl over to them.

But if they're too busy to heal you, all you're doing is putting yourself in the line of fire.

If you can reach some nearby cover, do that instead - make it hard for the opposition to eliminate you.

If you can't reach cover, keep your distance from teammates.

You're less likely to get hit by stray bullets, and you

might also divert your opponents' attention from the main battle.

Someone might try to eliminate you as you lie helpless, instead of concentrating their fire on your teammates who are the more dangerous ones.

But if you're the one who's just knocked down an opponent, don't fall into the same trap.

Yes, it can be tempting to eliminate opponents as soon as you knock them down.

No one wants to do all the hard work and then have a teammate walk up and deliver the last shot when your opponent can't fight back or run away.

But if you leave someone knocked out instead of eliminating them, then you can take advantage of the fact that teammates will generally want to revive each other.

Well, unless they don't like them very much!

(I must admit, I've left Leon on the battlefield a few times...)

If you're lucky, someone in the enemy squad will be tempted to go and heal their fallen comrade.

You'll have drawn them out of the main action - and you'll have a good chance to target them when they're out in the open!

CHAPTER 12

"So, I've decided whose idea we should go with," I tell our group when I get to school (before anyone can start talking about yesterday's disastrous Fortnite session and whose stupid idea it was!)

Maisie's eyes light up. So do Samson's.

OK....

Come on then, which one is it?

I let the suspense build up for a few moments, just to annoy them. (They deserve it.)

I point my finger...

...at Amy.

"What?" says Samson.

"What?" says Maisie.

"What?" says Amy when she notices everyone's looking at her.

"I want to go with Amy's idea," I say.

"But Amy doesn't have an idea," says Samson.

"How do we know? None of us ever asked her."

Maisie turns to Amy. "Do you have an idea?"

"No," says Amy as if ideas are for losers.

"Really?" I say. "You're sure nothing's been brewing in that brain of yours?"

"She doesn't want to," says Samson.

"Look - neither of you wants the other one to lead the team, and I had a go yesterday and that CLEARLY didn't work, so that leaves Amy."

Maisie opens her mouth to argue again, but then Amy says:

"Actually I did sort of have an idea."

"Great!" I say.

I hope it's not rubbish.

"I thought," Amy goes on, "maybe we could make, like, a vending machine."

Samson shakes his head. "That's far too complicated."

"It's not that hard," says Amy. "It can be a simple one with, like, three our four things in it. All you need is, like, a pivot at the back of the machine so when you push the button, it pushes the thing you want from behind, like, and it falls in the tray."

Amy grabs a piece of paper and starts to sketch some lines on it.

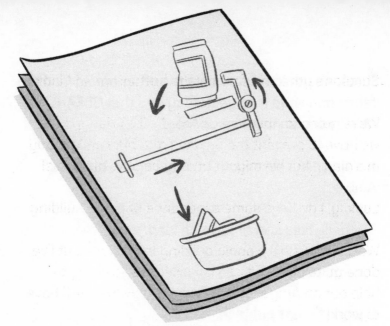

"But... could we even make that?" says Maisie.

"Course. It's just few bits of wood and some nails and maybe, like, some springs."

Amy draws more lines, and this does actually look like something we could make.

And it's not like anything any of the other groups are making.

"Have we got time?" asks Samson.

"Well we've got to make something."

Maisie's keen to design the casing for the machine.

Samson's got ideas for how the buttons should look.

We're going to have to work hard – it's Friday, and we have to present the finished machine on Monday morning – but we might actually be able to do this!

Luckily, I do have some experience of panic building.

Well, obviously it's panic building in Fortnite, but I've done quite a lot of it - so I'm excited and ready to help out on Amy's idea, no matter how fast we'll have to work!

Panic building protects you and frustrates your opponents.

Throwing up quick walls is the most basic type of panic structure, but there are ways to take this kind of building further without taking too much extra time over it, and if you practice you can assemble one really quickly.

Once the first storey of walls is in place, build a second storey.

If the enemy has a height advantage over you, one storey may not be enough.

Of course, by the time you've built the second storey, the enemy may have shot away your first one!

The **quick ramp** is another design you can develop.

Once your ramp is high enough (four stairways is usually about right), build walls on each side of the top stairway and another wall behind you on the ramp itself.

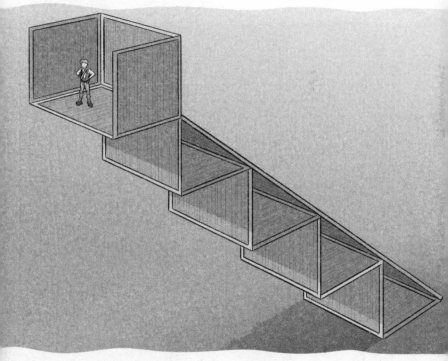

This wall blocks off the ramp to the rear.

The biggest risk on a ramp is an opponent following you up there and shooting you while you're looking the other way.

Placing a wall there gives you some protection, and it doesn't matter that you can't go back down your ramp - you can just jump off the end.

The panic fort is the simplest set of four walls with a roof.

Building a four-walled panic fort like that one is a good idea if you're concerned about being attacked while healing yourself or a teammate.

You can always adapt it into a more offensive fort when you've healed.

Always start building from your most vulnerable side.

If you're already under fire, this will be where the gunfire is coming from, but if not, start from the side an attack is most likely to come from.

And if you're not already under attack, this is a good moment to use stone or metal instead of wood - you've got a little more time to build and stronger materials will offer more protection.

If you're playing as a squad, being able to build something like this together is a real advantage - one of you can do the roof while another makes the walls.

The fort can also be adapted into a panic tower - and one of your squad can start working on it while you heal.

Instead of a roof, build four walls on top of the walls you've already got.

When you're all ready to move up into the tower, build a ramp, and then another ramp, and extend your fort upwards.

You can go as high as you like - but of course you can't move back down.

If you have a little breathing space, you can edit your ramps into staircases, which is hard to do quickly and under pressure.

This type of simple narrow tower can be adapted into a sniper tower.

The sniper tower involves placing a ramp at the top of each wall, spreading outwards.

Now you've got a vantage point in every direction, and your squad can try to pick off anyone approaching.

This offers a better range of views than just making a window, while also letting you dodge back behind the cover of the ramp if opponents return fire.

EXTRA HEIGHT ADVANTAGE. LESS BUILDING!

Building towers can burn through your resources quickly, so if you want to gain a height advantage without building too much, try making a sniper tower on top of an existing building.

Build your tower on the middle of a flat roof, preferably a large, high one, and build high enough to get a good view over the edge of the building.

The advantage of this is a lot of opponents won't see your fort until you start shooting - they'll be looking out for enemy structures on the ground, not on top of buildings.

And it's harder for them to strike back at you - they can't shoot away the base of your tower unless they climb on top of the building!

Another great use for a panic fort is to simply abandon it as soon as you've built it, and use it as a decoy.

Other players will often assume there's someone in the fort, and will focus their attention on it as they approach.

They will have no idea there is a sniper waiting to take them out!

Just make sure you hit them before they get inside - otherwise they may use your fort to gain an advantage over you!

CHAPTER 13

On Monday morning Amy, Maisie, Samson and I are in the corner of the classroom trying to put our machine together.

We finished making our all our individual bits over the weekend, but we haven't had a chance to actually check whether the whole thing works.

Maisie built and painted the box, Samson made the control panel, Amy made the mechanism, and I made the shelves and the things to go inside.

I hope we all got our measurements right - I was worrying Maisie would have measured hers in millimetres instead of centimetres or something...

"What are you doing over there?" says Ms Grimes from the front of the classroom.

"Just putting our project together," I say.

"It should already be together. Sit in your seats please."

The presentations begin with Sana's group - a multi-storey car park with lifts and barriers which raise when a car drives up to them.

They all stand around their model but Leon takes the lead, using the word 'I' a lot. "I really wanted it to do this... I thought it was important that..."

And so on, blah blah blah.

And then he picks up a toy car, rolls it over to the entrance barrier, which he just claimed he built himself - and nothing happens.

"Hang on..." he says and tries it again.

The barrier stays down. Leon rolls the car back and forth, getting more and more annoyed.

This is almost as fun as beating Leon at Fortnite.

"What's the problem, Leon?" asks Sana innocently.

"It's not working."

"So why don't you fix it?"

Leon looks down at the model. It's obvious he's got no idea how to fix it.

"Er..."

"Or maybe I should have a go?" Sana says, stepping forwards.

She lifts up a hatch in the road under the barrier, makes some adjustments and puts the hatch back down. She rolls the car up to the barrier... and the barrier raises.

"Very good, Sana," says Ms Grimes, "and the rest of your group."

Sana flashes a grin at me, and I smile back. She didn't sabotage her own model just so she could fix it, did she...?

But I can't hang around wondering about it, because we're up next...

Since it was Amy's idea, we've decided Amy should be the one to present it.

"So... er... this is, like, a vending machine, isn't it."

She points at the machine, which sits on a table in front of her. "And you can push the buttons and stuff comes out."

"What stuff comes out?" asks Ms Grimes.

"Like, this one gives you a drink," says Amy, pointing at a button. "This one gives you bandages, and this one gives you, er, a banana."

"What an odd collection of items."

"Tyler came up with those," says Maisie.

I don't tell Ms Grimes where I got the idea from... I don't think she'd approve.

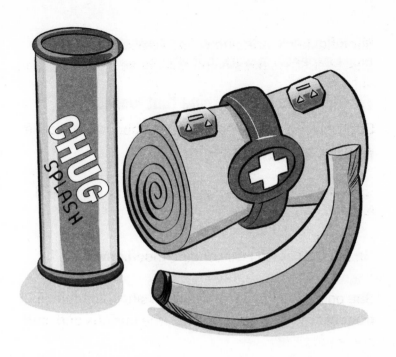

"So, can we see it in action?" asks Ms Grimes.

All the group look at each other. No-one dares press a button.

"I'll do it," I say, because I'm feeling pretty brave. Or reckless.

I step forward, push the picture of a can...

And a can comes out of the bottom!

My team cheers, which sort of gives away that we didn't expect it to work, but who cares.

We did it! We made a thing that works!

And it's all thanks to Fortnite!

Sort of.

On my way home I drop in on Alfie - I haven't seen him since I shouted at him for getting on my nerves during the big battle, and I should probably apologise.

Also, I want to hear how he and Ellie got on at their tournament at the weekend.

I was going to ask Ellie today at school, but I didn't see her, it was almost like she was avoiding me...

I go round the back and find the door open - he won't mind if I just let myself in, I do it all the time.

"Alfie, it's me!" I shout as I walk in - I can hear the TV's on, sounds like Captain Marvel...

I step into the living room -

And Alfie's on the sofa.

With Ellie.

And their arms around each other.

"Oh," says Alfie. "Hi, Tyler."

"Wait... are you two –"

Ellie glances up at me.

"Look, Tyler, don't make a big deal of it," she says.

"Er... OK," I say. "How did your tournament go?"

Ellie and Alfie talk over each other:

"Really well – quarter-finals," says Alfie.

"Really badly – quarter-finals," says Ellie.

"Cool," I say, nodding. "Cool, cool, cool. Er... Alfie... Sorry I had a go at you the other day."

"Oh sure, whatever," says Alfie.

Ellie elbows him in the ribs and he adds, "Er, and sorry I was annoying."

"S'alright. Playing with that lot made me realise what a proper team's like. Like us lot."

"Funny you should say that," says Ellie. "We were thinking of entering a Squads tournament next time, if you and Sana wanna join to make up the four?"

"Yeah, why not?" I say.

"Hey, it'll be like a double date!" says Alfie.

Will it...??

I can feel myself going red in the face, but I guess the four of us do make a good squad - Sana's strategy, Ellie's marksmanship, Alfie's building and my... whatever I bring.

"OK," I tell them. "I'm up for it."

Maybe as we go along, I'll find what I'm actually good at? I've learned it's not leadership, anyway.

"One thing, though," says Ellie.

"Yeah," says Alfie, "Ellie and me have been talking and..."

"What?" I ask.

"Don't take this the wrong way, but -"

"You have to do something about your skin," says Ellie.

"My skin?" I reach up to my face, wondering whether I'm still bright red, or whether I'm covered in spots? Why didn't anyone tell me before?

"Yeah, we are *not* entering a tournament with you playing in the noob skin."

'Oh, my *Fortnite* skin!'

"No offence, but you look like an amateur in that thing."

"Maybe that's good! Maybe the opposition will underestimate us?"

Alfie shakes his head. "They'll just target us."

"What does Sana think?"

"She agrees with me," says Ellie quickly. "She's just too nice to say it."

"And you're not?"

"Absolutely not, no. If you want to be on the squad, you need a proper skin. OK?"

"OK," I say, grinning.

A real Fortnite tournament?

Did things just get serious...?

FIND OUT WHAT HAPPENS NEXT, IN...

SECRETS OF A FORTNITE FAN:
LLAMA DRAMA

Tyler and his friends
team up to take on the ULTIMATE
FORTNITE CHALLENGE!

COMING SOON!

ALSO AVAILABLE

TYLER'S FIRST FORTNITE ADVENTURE